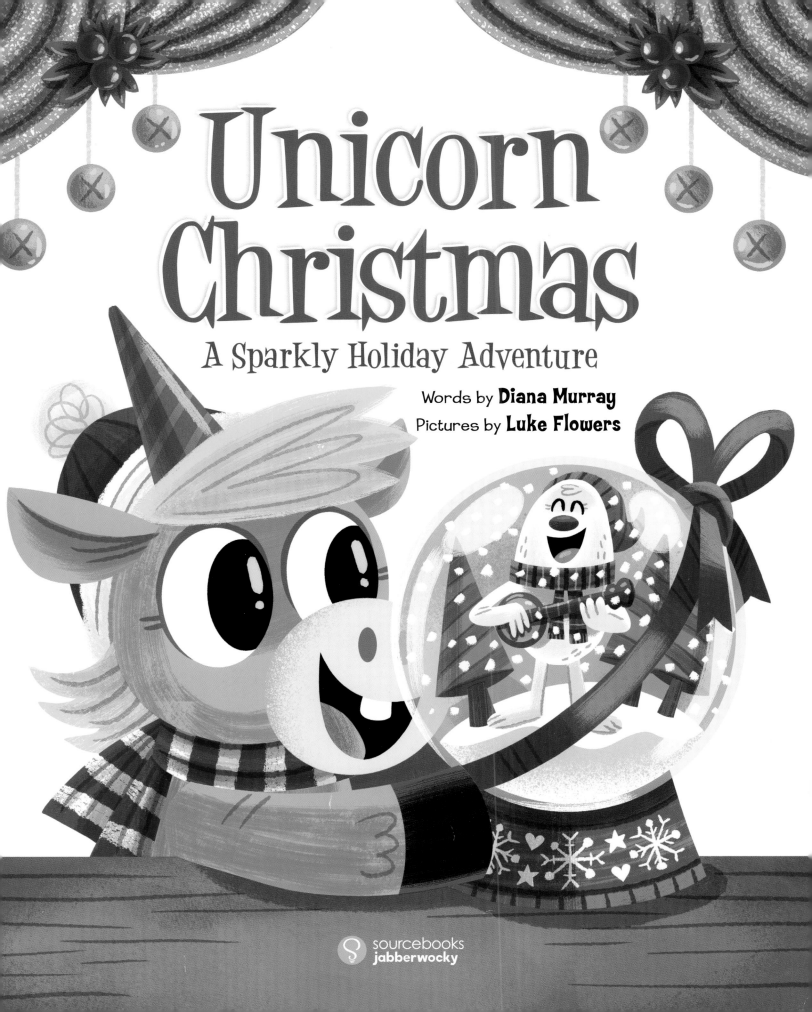

Unicorn Christmas

A Sparkly Holiday Adventure

Words by **Diana Murray**
Pictures by **Luke Flowers**

sourcebooks
jabberwocky

For Danny, Kat, and Jane.
—DM

For Matt Kaufenberg. The inspiration, laughter and friendship you've
blessed me with through the years is truly a treasured gift.
Wishing you and your sweet crew a festive holiday season
with ice cream salads and cozy storytimes.
—LF

Text © 2022 by Diana Murray • Illustrations © 2022 by Luke Flowers • Cover and internal design © 2022 by Sourcebooks •
Sourcebooks and the colophon are registered trademarks of Sourcebooks. • All rights reserved. • The characters and events
portrayed in this book are fictitious or are used fictitiously. Any similarity to real persons, living or dead, is purely coincidental
and not intended by the author. • The full color art was sketched and painted in Photoshop using a wide range of unique digital
brushes. • Published by Sourcebooks Jabberwocky, an imprint of Sourcebooks Kids • P.O. Box 4410, Naperville, Illinois
60567-4410 • (630) 961-3900 • sourcebookskids.com • Cataloging-in-Publication Data is on file with the Library of Congress.
• Source of Production: Worzalla, Stevens Point, Wisconsin, USA • Date of Production: July 2022 • Run Number: 5024691

It's Christmas Eve!
A magic night
when forests glow
with twinkling light.

Unicorns
this time of year
are busy spreading
Christmas cheer!

They send out cards
by shooting star...
to friends and neighbors
near and far,

decorate!

They trim a tree
with lollipops,
with butterflies,
and lemon drops,

and rainbow flowers
on a string.
With jolly neighs,
they start to sing:

Sparkly Snowflakes, candy canes,
velvet ribbons tied in manes.
Jingle-jingle! Neigh, neigh, neigh!
Clap your hooves for Christmas Day!

Next, the presents.
Time to wrap!
With magic horns,
they point and ZAP!

A fancy brush
for Mermaid's hair.

For Yeti?
Long wool underwear.

For Dragon?
Coins inside a chest.

They guess what each
friend might like best.

They whip up pies
and cakes to eat,
and one real
extra special treat.

A crispy batch
of gingercorns

with swirly icing
on the horns!

They sprinkle
fairy dust on top...
and off the cookies
skip and hop!

The guests arrive
and one by one,
they join the festive
party fun!

Dancing, prancing,
cookie-chasing,

carol-singing,
ice-skate-racing,

snow-tube-riding
down a hill,
all goes just as planned,
until…

They hear a jingle
overhead
and see a flying
Christmas sled!

The final party guests are here! It's Santa and his eight reindeer!

He lands the sled,
reins in his crew,
and starts to wave,
when… "Ah-ahh-choooooooo!"

uh-oh.

Santa's sick!
So tired, he's dizzy.
"Can't stay long,"
he sighs. "Too busy."

"Got to hurry
on our way.
No time to rest
'til Christmas Day!"

His reindeer crew
looks weary too…

But unicorns
can help them through!

They lighten
Santa's load of toys,
flying gifts
to girls and boys.

Santa can't believe his eyes! They're finished long before sunrise!

They take him home
and tuck him in.
He thanks them with
a whiskered grin.

They fly back through a wintry storm.

Although it's cold,
their hearts feel warm.

The forest sparkles
snowy white
as unicorns
get snuggled tight

and share a cup
of fairy tea,
tired but cozy
as can be.

As snow piles up
twelve inches deep,
the unicorns
fall fast asleep.

On Christmas morning,
rubbing eyes,
they wake up to...

a big surprise!

Santa's back!
The reindeer too!
They're full of spunk
and good as new.

And thanks to all that rest last night, they're ready for…

Kapowww!

Snowball

Bells on horns
and antlers ring
as joyful friends
hold hooves and sing:

Sparkly Snowflakes, candy canes,
velvet ribbons tied in manes.
Jingle-jingle! Neigh, neigh, neigh!
Clap your hooves for Christmas Day!